FATHER CHRISTMAS

Other books
by Raymond Briggs

FATHER CHRISTMAS GOES ON HOLIDAY
JIM AND THE BEANSTALK
FUNGUS THE BOGEYMAN
THE SNOWMAN

Based on Raymond Briggs' original story

THE SNOWMAN AND THE SNOWDOG BOOK AND CD

Raymond Briggs
Father Christmas

PUFFIN

For my Mother and Father

PUFFIN BOOKS
Published by the Penguin Group: London, New York, Australia, Canada, India,
Ireland, New Zealand and South Africa
Penguin Books Ltd, Registered Offices: 80 Strand, London WC2R 0RL, England
puffinbooks.com
First published by Hamish Hamilton 1973
Published in Puffin Books 1974
This edition published 2013
006
Copyright © Raymond Briggs, 1973
All rights reserved
The moral right of the author/illustrator has been asserted
Made and printed in China
ISBN: 978–0–723–27797–2

Father Christmas

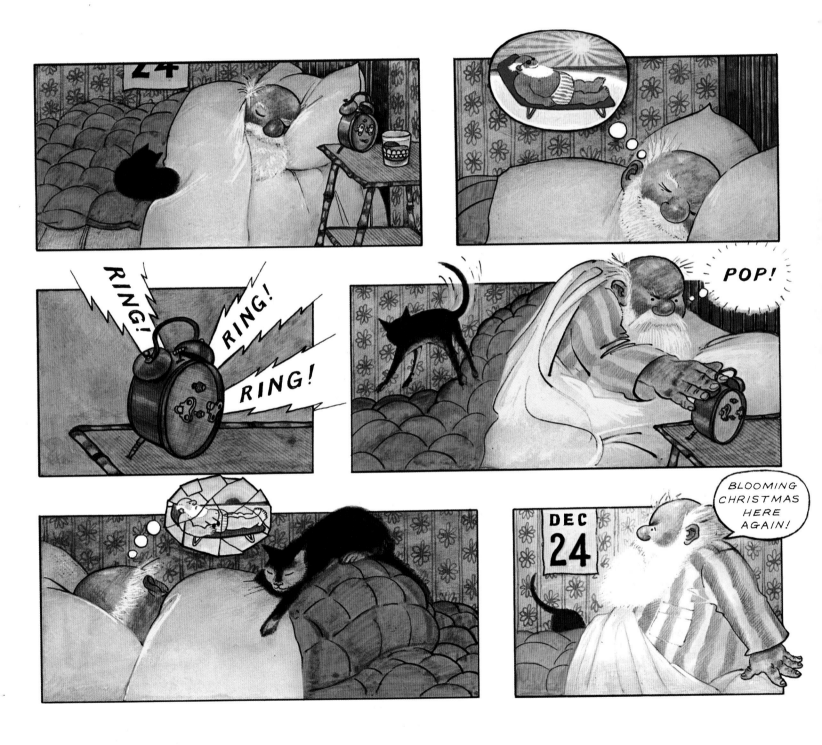

KEEP STILL YOU SILLY DEERS !

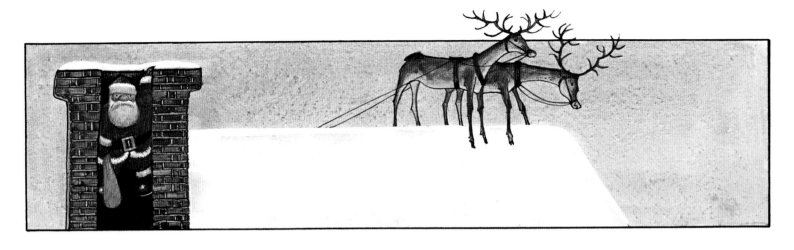

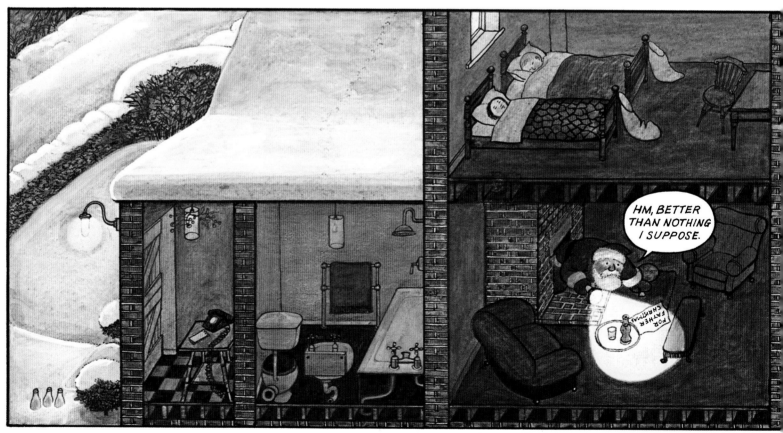

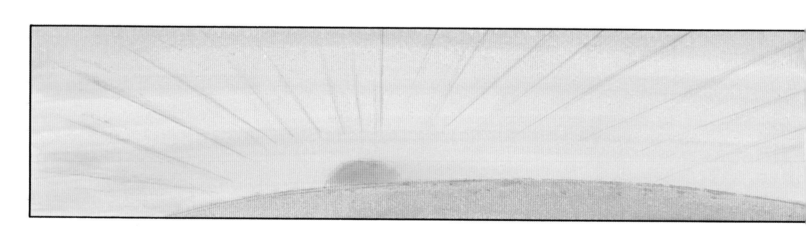

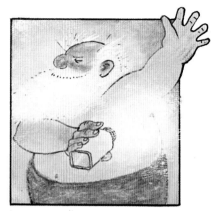

BLOOMING AWFUL TIE FROM AUNTY ELSIE!

HORRIBLE SOCKS FROM COUSIN VIOLET!

AH! THAT'S MORE LIKE IT. GOOD OLD FRED!

The End